W9-ARA-404

We dedicate this book to the employees at all of the Homewood Suites
by Hilton hotels around the world – you are our heroes!

We also dedicate this to our families, the Duncans and the Epps.
And finally to our loving and wonderful wife and mother, Julie, who
inspires us every day – and puts up with our bickering back and forth!!!

Copyright © 2010 Hilton Worldwide

HWS Publishing

ISBN 978-0-9815285-3-3
ISBN 0-9815285-3-8

How This Book Took Flight

Bill: So my son comes to me one day and says, "Dad, I'm proud of you for writing these books, but you need to make 'em more interesting. Maybe one from the kids' point of view." Interesting concept, I thought, once the sting of the backhanded compliment subsided (teenagers!). And since it was Christian's idea, I drafted him to help out. This book is the culmination of that conversation – if you can call it a conversation.

Christian: I really liked the first two Lewis books, and had an idea to mix it up a bit by having the kids plan part of their trip, from a teen's perspective. Personally, I love to travel – always have, and always will. Hope all you duck lovers out there enjoy!

Lewis the Duck was sitting at his desk one day. He was daydreaming. "I am ready for my next big adventure," he said to himself. Out of the blue, Mr. Wood called for him to come to his office right away.

"There's a big meeting in Mexico, and I can't make it. You're a duck I have my full trust in, so I want you to fill in for me."

"That's great, Mr. Wood. I'd love to go! I hear Mexico is nice this time of year," said Lewis.

Mr. Wood had a great idea: "I know the kids are out of school on break, so why not make this another family vacation?" he asked. "This could be another exciting adventure for you and your family, Lewis."

"I'm sure they will love to go; what a great idea! Thank you, sir, and I promise to put my best 'foot' forward. I won't let you down," said Lewis.

"I know you won't," said Mr. Wood, "and that's why I picked you!" Mr. Wood exclaimed. "You'd better get flying!"

Later that night, Lewis told his wife, Lois, and his two kids, Lance and Lisa, about their trip to Mexico. "That sounds exciting! I have friends that have been, and they say it's wonderful!" said Lois.

"Well, get packing! We leave first thing in the morning!" said Lewis.

W hile Lewis was packing, Lisa and Lance came to see him. "Dad, since we are a little older now, may Lance and I plan part of our trip?" asked Lisa. Lance chimed in, "That would be so cool – see Mexico from a bird's-eye view. There are so many fun things to do." Lewis thought for a moment, talked to his wife, Lois, and then told the kids, "Have at it, but just make sure you work around my meetings." "Yeah!" shouted Lisa and Lance together.

"Kids, why don't you find that project you did last year on Mexico? I think if you look at it, you will find you have a good bit of the trip planned out," said Lois.

"Good idea, Mom," replied Lisa and Lance. Turns out Mrs. Duck was right. . . .

The 15th largest
country in the world
•
Independence Day:
September 16, 1810
•
Mexico is home to over
100 Million People

Capital City:
Mexico City

Official Language:
Spanish

They packed, put together their list and were soon off. After crossing the border in Tijuana – the Gateway to Mexico – the Duck family made their way to their favorite hotel away from home, Homewood Suites by Hilton. They unpacked, settled in and got a good night's rest – after all, they had a busy vacation planned after Lewis' meetings.

And a great vacation they had. The Duck family really enjoyed their time in the water. They went snorkeling in Cancun, scuba diving in Cabo San Lucas and enjoyed the white sandy beaches of Acapulco and Cozumel. While there, they saw one of the world's largest coral reefs.

T

hey shopped in Guadalajara, attended a Mexican Day of Independence

celebration in Mexico City, traveled the countryside on the Chihuahua-Pacific

Railway and saw Popocatépetl, an active volcano near the city of Puebla.

Because ducks can travel great distances, they were able to make it back to their favorite hotel every night. Homewood Suites was a nest away from home where they could relax and get ready for more adventures each day.

They visited Mayan and Aztec ruins and hiked through tropical forests.

They even saw several soccer games. Soccer is the most popular sport in Mexico.

O n their last night, Lewis, Lois and the kids treated themselves to a delicious Mexican dinner of fresh seafood, vegetables, tortillas, rice and beans. Lisa was delighted when a trio of mariachis played at their table!

The Duck family was glad to get home, but they won't forget the many exciting things they did in Mexico.

Lewis was pleased, for his dream of an adventure had come true! As he slept that night, Lewis wondered where his next adventure would take him.

Author Bios:
This is Bill Duncan's third book in the Lewis the Duck series, that includes *Lewis The Duck and His Long Trip* and *Lewis The Duck Goes to Canada*. He lives in Memphis, Tennessee, with his wife, Julie, and son, Christian.

Christian Duncan lives in Memphis, Tennessee, with his above mentioned parents and his three dogs, Seth, Mary Margaret and Barnabas. A sophomore in high school, this is his first book.

Artist Bio:
Greg Cravens is the creator of the syndicated cartoon *The Buckets*, *Lewis The Duck and His Long Trip* and *Lewis The Duck Goes to Canada*. He enjoys spending time with his wife, Paula, and sons, Gideon and Cory.

The Story of
Lewis

Our guests often ask, "Why the duck?
Who is he and what does a duck have to do with Homewood Suites?"

Homewood Suites chose a duck because it symbolizes versatility and adaptability. Ducks are comfortable in air, in water and on land. They migrate long distances over extended periods. And their ability to adapt and thrive in a variety of places represents our goal in the travel and hospitality industry – to serve guests with resourcefulness and flexibility.

We chose a wood duck, considered one of the most beautiful creatures in nature. And we've given him a name – Lewis. By naming Lewis and bringing him to life, we've created a visual representation of a unique brand that caters to those who want the comforts of home when on the road for a few days or more. And, with Lewis to guide us, there is no doubt that we will meet our guests' individual needs for comfort, flexibility and convenience.

HOMEWOOD
SUITES
—— Hilton ——